Published by
SelfMadeHero
A division of Metro Media Ltd
5 Upper Wimpole Street
London W1G 6BP
www.selfmadehero.com

This edition published 2009

Illustrator: Faye Yong
Text Adaptor: Richard Appignanesi
Designer: Andy Huckle
Textual Consultant: Nick de Somogyi
Publishing Director: Emma Hayley
With thanks to: Doug Wallace

ISBN: 978-0-9558169-1-8

10 9 8 7 6 5 4 3 2 1
Printed and bound in China

MANGA SHAKESPEARE ®

THE MERCHANT OF VENICE

ADAPTED BY

RICHARD APPIGNANESI

ILLUSTRATED BY

FAYE YONG

Portia, a wealthy heiress of Belmont

"O, these deliberate fools!"

"Silence bestows virtue, Madam!"

Nerissa, her maid

Stephano and Balthasar,
two messengers

"I bring word!"

Leonardo, servant to Bassanio

The Prince of Aragon, suitor to Portia

"What's here?
The portrait of a
blinking idiot!"

"Mislike me
not for my
complexion..."

The Prince of Morocco, suitor to Portia

"What news on the Rialto?"

Venice

YOUR MIND IS TOSSING ON THE OCEAN, WHERE YOUR ARGOSIES WITH PORTLY SAIL,

LIKE PAGEANTS OF THE SEA, DO OVERPEER THE PETTY TRAFFICKERS.

BELIEVE ME, SIR, HAD I SUCH VENTURE FORTH,

I SHOULD BE PEERING FOR EVERY OBJECT THAT MIGHT MAKE ME FEAR MISFORTUNE TO MY VENTURES.

SHOULD I GO TO CHURCH AND SEE THE HOLY STONE, AND NOT THINK OF DANGEROUS ROCKS, WHICH, TOUCHING MY VESSEL'S SIDE,

WOULD SCATTER ALL HER SPICES ON THE STREAM, ENROBE THE WATERS WITH MY SILKS...

AND NOW WORTH NOTHING?

I KNOW ANTONIO IS SAD TO THINK UPON HIS MERCHANDISE.

THEN LET US SAY YOU ARE SAD BECAUSE YOU ARE NOT MERRY.

AND 'TWERE AS EASY FOR YOU TO LAUGH, AND SAY YOU ARE MERRY BECAUSE YOU ARE NOT SAD.

HERE COMES BASSANIO, YOUR MOST NOBLE KINSMAN,

GRATIANO AND LORENZO.

WE LEAVE YOU NOW WITH BETTER COMPANY.

I WOULD HAVE STAYED TILL I HAD MADE YOU MERRY.

YOUR WORTH IS VERY DEAR IN MY REGARD.

GOOD SIGNIORS, WHEN SHALL WE LAUGH? SAY, WHEN?

YOU GROW EXCEEDING STRANGE.

WE'LL MAKE OUR LEISURES TO ATTEND ON YOURS.

MY LORD BASSANIO, SINCE YOU HAVE FOUND ANTONIO, WE TWO WILL LEAVE YOU.

BUT AT DINNER-TIME, I PRAY YOU HAVE IN MIND WHERE WE MUST MEET.

I WILL NOT FAIL YOU.

YOU LOOK NOT WELL, SIGNIOR ANTONIO.

BELIEVE ME, YOU ARE MARVELLOUSLY CHANGED.

I HOLD THE WORLD BUT AS A STAGE WHERE EVERY MAN MUST PLAY A PART...

AND MINE A SAD ONE.

MY PURSE, MY PERSON, MY EXTREMEST MEANS, LIE ALL UNLOCKED TO YOUR OCCASIONS.

I OWE YOU MUCH, AND LIKE A WILFUL YOUTH, THAT WHICH I OWE IS LOST.

BUT IF YOU PLEASE TO SHOOT ANOTHER ARROW THAT WAY WHICH YOU DID SHOOT THE FIRST, I WILL AIM TO FIND BOTH, OR BRING YOUR LATTER HAZARD BACK AGAIN,

AND THANKFULLY REST DEBTOR FOR THE FIRST.

IS IT NOT HARD, NERISSA, THAT I CANNOT CHOOSE ONE, NOR REFUSE NONE?

YOUR FATHER WAS EVER VIRTUOUS.

THEREFORE THE LOTTERY THAT HE HATH DEVISED IN THESE THREE CHESTS OF GOLD, SILVER AND LEAD,

WHEREOF WHO CHOOSES HIS MEANING CHOOSES *YOU*...

WILL NEVER BE CHOSEN BY ANY RIGHTLY BUT ONE WHO YOU SHALL RIGHTLY LOVE.

BUT WHAT WARMTH IS THERE IN YOUR AFFECTION TOWARDS ANY OF THESE PRINCELY SUITORS THAT ARE ALREADY COME?

I PRAY THEE, AS THOU NAMEST THEM, I WILL DESCRIBE THEM.

FIRST, THERE IS THE NEAPOLITAN PRINCE.

AY, THAT'S A COLT INDEED — FOR HE DOTH NOTHING BUT TALK OF HIS HORSE.

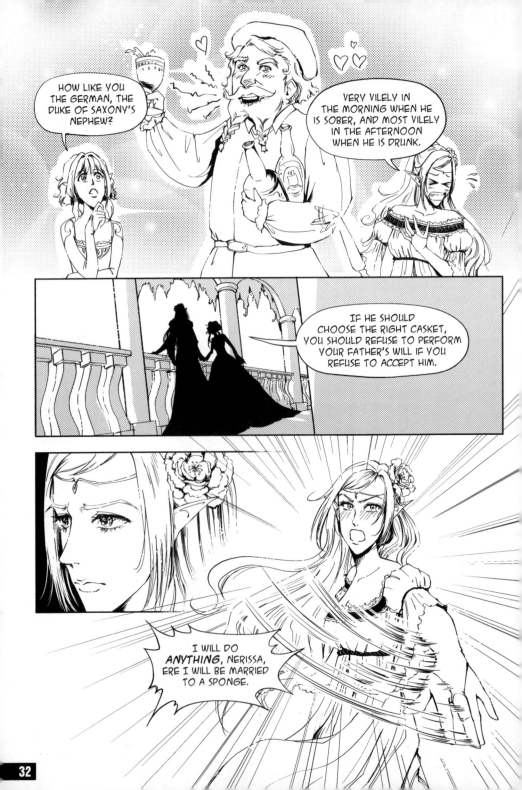

HOW LIKE YOU THE GERMAN, THE DUKE OF SAXONY'S NEPHEW?

VERY VILELY IN THE MORNING WHEN HE IS SOBER, AND MOST VILELY IN THE AFTERNOON WHEN HE IS DRUNK.

IF HE SHOULD CHOOSE THE RIGHT CASKET, YOU SHOULD REFUSE TO PERFORM YOUR FATHER'S WILL IF YOU REFUSE TO ACCEPT HIM.

I WILL DO *ANYTHING*, NERISSA, ERE I WILL BE MARRIED TO A SPONGE.

YOU NEED NOT FEAR, LADY.

THEY HAVE ACQUAINTED ME WITH THEIR DETERMINATION TO RETURN TO THEIR HOME AND TROUBLE YOU NO MORE...

UNLESS YOU MAY BE WON BY SOME OTHER SORT THAN YOUR FATHER'S CASKETS.

I WILL DIE AS CHASTE AS DIANA UNLESS I BE OBTAINED BY THE MANNER OF MY FATHER'S WILL.

DO YOU NOT REMEMBER...

IN YOUR FATHER'S TIME,

A VENETIAN, A SCHOLAR AND A SOLDIER, THAT CAME HITHER IN COMPANY OF THE MARQUIS OF MONTFERRAT?

YES, YES, IT WAS BASSANIO.

HE, OF ALL THE MEN, WAS THE BEST DESERVING A FAIR LADY.

I REMEMBER HIM WORTHY OF THY PRAISE.

ANTONIO IS A GOOD MAN.

HAVE YOU HEARD TO THE CONTRARY?

HO, NO, NO! MY MEANING IS THAT HE IS SUFFICIENT. YET HIS MEANS ARE IN SUPPOSITION.

HE HATH AN ARGOSY BOUND TO TRIPOLIS, ANOTHER TO THE INDIES, A THIRD AT MEXICO, A FOURTH FOR ENGLAND, AND OTHER VENTURES ABROAD.

I HATE HIM FOR HE IS A CHRISTIAN.

BUT MORE FOR THAT HE LENDS OUT MONEY GRATIS, AND BRINGS DOWN THE RATE OF USANCE HERE WITH US IN VENICE.

IF I CAN CATCH HIM ONCE, I WILL FEED FAT THE ANCIENT GRUDGE I BEAR HIM.

CURSED BE MY TRIBE IF I FORGIVE HIM!

I CANNOT INSTANTLY RAISE UP THE GROSS OF FULL THREE THOUSAND DUCATS.

WHAT OF THAT? TUBAL, A WEALTHY HEBREW OF MY TRIBE, WILL FURNISH ME.

HOW MANY MONTHS DO YOU DESIRE?

SHYLOCK, ALBEIT I NEITHER LEND NOR BORROW BY TAKING NOR BY GIVING OF EXCESS...

YET I'LL BREAK A CUSTOM.

YOU THAT DID FOOT ME AS YOU SPURN A STRANGER CUR.

IS IT POSSIBLE A *CUR* CAN LEND THREE THOUSAND DUCATS?

OR SHALL I BEND LOW AND WITH HUMBLENESS SAY THIS —

"FAIR SIR, YOU SPAT ON ME, CALLED ME DOG, AND FOR THESE COURTESIES I'LL LEND YOU THUS MUCH MONEYS"?

I AM AS LIKE TO CALL THEE SO AGAIN.

IF THOU WILT LEND THIS MONEY, LEND IT NOT AS TO THY FRIENDS, BUT RATHER TO THINE *ENEMY*,

WHO IF HE BREAK, THOU MAYST WITH BETTER FACE EXACT THE PENALTY.

I WOULD BE *FRIENDS* WITH YOU AND SUPPLY YOUR PRESENT WANTS, AND TAKE NO USANCE FOR MY MONEYS.

THIS IS *KIND* I OFFER.

THIS WERE *KINDNESS*.

YES, SHYLOCK, I WILL SEAL UNTO THIS BOND.

THEN MEET ME FORTHWITH AT THE NOTARY'S.

I LIKE NOT FAIR TERMS AND A VILLAIN'S MIND.

COME ON. IN THIS THERE CAN BE NO DISMAY. MY SHIPS COME HOME A MONTH BEFORE THE DAY.

CAN YOU TELL ME WHETHER ONE LAUNCELOT DWELLS WITH HIM OR NO?

TALK NOT OF MASTER LAUNCELOT, FOR THE YOUNG GENTLEMAN IS INDEED... DECEASED.

GOD FORBID! THE BOY WAS THE VERY STAFF OF MY AGE.

DO YOU KNOW ME, FATHER?

ALACK, SIR, I AM SAND-BLIND.

...

O RARE FORTUNE! HERE COMES THE MAN!

HERE'S MY SON, SIR, A POOR BOY—

NOT A POOR BOY, SIR, BUT THE RICH JEW'S MAN, THAT WOULD—

AS ONE WOULD SAY, TO SERVE—

AS MY FATHER SHALL SPECIFY—

SERVE YOU, SIR.

ONE SPEAK FOR BOTH. WHAT WOULD YOU?

THOU HAST OBTAINED THY SUIT. SHYLOCK SPOKE WITH ME THIS DAY AND HATH PREFERRED THEE...

IF IT BE PREFERMENT TO LEAVE A RICH JEW'S SERVICE TO BECOME THE FOLLOWER OF SO POOR A GENTLEMAN.

IF I DO NOT PUT ON A SOBER HABIT AND USE ALL THE OBSERVANCE OF CIVILITY, LIKE ONE WELL STUDIED TO PLEASE HIS GRANDAM...

NEVER TRUST ME MORE.

WELL, WE SHALL SEE YOUR BEARING.

NAY, BUT YOU SHALL NOT GAUGE ME BY WHAT WE DO TONIGHT.

NO, I WOULD ENTREAT YOU RATHER TO PUT ON YOUR BOLDEST SUIT OF MIRTH, FOR WE HAVE FRIENDS THAT PURPOSE MERRIMENT.

ALACK, WHAT HEINOUS SIN IS IT IN ME TO BE ASHAMED TO BE MY FATHER'S CHILD!

BUT THOUGH I AM A DAUGHTER TO HIS BLOOD...

I AM NOT TO HIS MANNERS.

O LORENZO! IF THOU KEEP PROMISE, I SHALL END THIS STRIFE...

BECOME A CHRISTIAN AND THY LOVING WIFE.

I AM RIGHT LOATH TO GO. THERE IS SOME ILL A-BREWING TOWARDS MY REST, FOR I DID DREAM OF MONEY-BAGS TONIGHT.

I BESEECH YOU, SIR, GO. I WILL NOT SAY YOU SHALL SEE A MASQUE...

WHAT! ARE THERE MASQUES?

HEAR ME, JESSICA.

LOCK UP MY DOORS. CLAMBER NOT UP, NOR THRUST YOUR HEAD INTO THE STREET TO GAZE ON CHRISTIAN FOOLS WITH VARNISHED FACES.

MISTRESS, LOOK OUT AT WINDOW...

FOR THERE WILL COME A CHRISTIAN WORTH A JEWESS' EYE.

WHAT SAYS THAT FOOL?

"FAREWELL, MISTRESS" — NOTHING ELSE.

DRONES HIVE NOT WITH ME. THEREFORE I PART WITH HIM TO ONE THAT I WOULD HAVE HIM HELP TO *WASTE* HIS BORROWED PURSE.

DO AS I BID YOU, SHUT DOORS AFTER YOU.

FAREWELL...

AND IF MY FORTUNE BE NOT CROSSED, I HAVE A FATHER, YOU A DAUGHTER, LOST.

SWEET FRIENDS,
APPROACH. HERE
DWELLS MY FATHER
JEW.

HO!
WHO'S
WITHIN?

WHO ARE YOU?
TELL ME, ALBEIT I'LL
SWEAR THAT I DO
KNOW YOUR
TONGUE.

LORENZO,
AND THY
LOVE.

HOW SHALL I KNOW IF I DO CHOOSE THE RIGHT?

ONE OF THEM CONTAINS MY PICTURE. IF YOU CHOOSE THAT, THEN I AM YOURS.

WHO CHOOSETH ME MUST GIVE AND HAZARD ALL HE HATH.

LET ME SEE AGAIN. WHAT SAYS THIS LEADEN CASKET? "WHO CHOOSETH ME MUST *GIVE* AND *HAZARD* ALL HE HATH."

MEN THAT HAZARD ALL DO IT IN HOPE OF FAIR ADVANTAGES.

WHO CHOOSETH ME SHALL GAIN
WHAT MANY MEN DESIRE.

"WHO CHOOSETH ME SHALL GAIN WHAT MANY MEN DESIRE." WHY, *THAT'S* THE LADY!

ALL THE WORLD DESIRES HER. FROM THE FOUR CORNERS OF THE EARTH THEY COME.

NEVER SO RICH A GEM WAS SET IN WORSE THAN *GOLD*.

HERE AN ANGEL IN A GOLDEN BED LIES ALL WITHIN.

COLD INDEED, AND LABOUR LOST.

PORTIA, ADIEU! I HAVE TOO *GRIEVED* A HEART TO TAKE A TEDIOUS LEAVE. THUS LOSERS PART.

A GENTLE RIDDANCE.

DRAW THE CURTAINS, GO. LET ALL OF HIS COMPLEXION CHOOSE ME SO.

I SAW BASSANIO UNDER SAIL. WITH HIM IS GRATIANO GONE ALONG — AND IN THEIR SHIP I AM SURE LORENZO IS NOT.

THE JEW WITH OUTCRIES RAISED THE DUKE TO SEARCH BASSANIO'S SHIP.

HE CAME TOO LATE. IN A GONDOLA WERE SEEN TOGETHER LORENZO AND HIS AMOROUS JESSICA.

I NEVER HEARD A PASSION SO *CONFUSED* AS THE JEW DID UTTER IN THE STREETS —

THE PRINCE OF ARAGON COMES TO HIS ELECTION.

BEHOLD — THERE STAND THE CASKETS, NOBLE PRINCE.

IF YOU CHOOSE THAT WHEREIN I AM CONTAINED, STRAIGHT SHALL OUR NUPTIAL RITES BE SOLEMNIZED.

BUT IF YOU *FAIL*, YOU MUST BE GONE FROM HENCE IMMEDIATELY.

I AM ENJOINED BY OATH, FIRST, NEVER TO UNFOLD TO ANYONE WHICH CASKET 'TWAS I CHOSE.

NEXT, IF I FAIL OF THE RIGHT CASKET, NEVER IN MY LIFE TO WOO A MAID IN WAY OF MARRIAGE.

TO THESE INJUNCTIONS EVERYONE DOTH SWEAR THAT COMES TO HAZARD FOR MY WORTHLESS SELF.

WHY THEN, TO THEE, THOU *SILVER* TREASURE HOUSE.

"WHO CHOOSETH ME SHALL GET AS MUCH AS HE *DESERVES.*"

AND WELL SAID TOO! GIVE ME A KEY FOR THIS.

WITH *ONE* FOOL'S HEAD I CAME TO WOO, BUT I GO AWAY WITH *TWO*.

SWEET, ADIEU! I'LL KEEP MY OATH, PATIENTLY TO BEAR MY WROTH.

THUS HATH THE CANDLE SINGED THE MOTH.

O, THESE DELIBERATE *FOOLS!* WHEN THEY DO CHOOSE, THEY HAVE THE WISDOM BY THEIR WIT TO LOSE.

THE ANCIENT SAYING IS NO HERESY: "HANGING AND WIVING GOES BY DESTINY".

WHERE IS MY LADY?

MADAM, THERE IS ALIGHTED AT YOUR GATE A YOUNG VENETIAN...

ONE THAT COMES TO SIGNIFY THE APPROACHING OF HIS LORD...

FROM WHOM HE BRINGETH *GIFTS* OF RICH VALUE.

COME, NERISSA, FOR I LONG TO SEE QUICK CUPID'S POST THAT COMES SO MANNERLY.

BASSANIO, LORD LOVE, IF THY WILL IT BE!

THERE IS MORE DIFFERENCE BETWEEN THY FLESH AND HERS THAN BETWEEN JET AND IVORY.

BUT DO YOU HEAR WHETHER ANTONIO HAVE HAD ANY LOSS AT SEA OR NO?

THERE I HAVE ANOTHER BAD MATCH! A *BANKRUPT* WHO DARE SCARCE SHOW HIS HEAD ON THE RIALTO.

HE WAS WONT TO CALL ME *USURER*. LET HIM LOOK TO HIS BOND!

IF A JEW WRONG A CHRISTIAN, WHAT IS HIS HUMILITY?

REVENGE.

SMACK

IF A CHRISTIAN WRONG A JEW, WHAT SHOULD HIS SUFFERANCE BE BY CHRISTIAN EXAMPLE?

WHY, *REVENGE!*

THE *VILLAINY* YOU TEACH ME I WILL EXECUTE.

HERE COMES ANOTHER OF THE TRIBE.

TUBAL!

WHAT NEWS FROM GENOA? HAST THOU FOUND MY DAUGHTER?

I OFTEN CAME WHERE I DID HEAR OF HER, BUT CANNOT FIND HER.

A DIAMOND GONE COST ME TWO THOUSAND DUCATS — AND OTHER PRECIOUS JEWELS...

I WOULD MY DAUGHTER WERE **DEAD** AT MY FOOT AND THE JEWELS IN HER EAR!

YOUR DAUGHTER SPENT IN GENOA, ONE NIGHT, *FOURSCORE* DUCATS.

THOU STICK'ST A *DAGGER* IN ME. I SHALL NEVER SEE MY GOLD AGAIN.

THERE CAME ANTONIO'S CREDITORS TO VENICE THAT SWEAR HE CANNOT CHOOSE BUT *BREAK*.

I AM VERY *GLAD* OF IT.

ONE OF THEM SHOWED ME A **RING** THAT HE HAD OF YOUR DAUGHTER FOR A **MONKEY.**

IT WAS MY **TURQUOISE.**

I HAD IT OF **LEAH** WHEN I WAS A BACHELOR.

I WOULD NOT HAVE GIVEN IT FOR A **WILDERNESS** OF MONKEYS.

BUT ANTONIO IS CERTAINLY *UNDONE*.

THAT'S VERY TRUE.

GO, TUBAL, FEE ME AN OFFICER. I WILL HAVE THE *HEART* OF HIM IF HE FORFEIT.

GO, TUBAL, AND MEET ME AT OUR SYNAGOGUE.

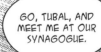

I PRAY YOU PAUSE BEFORE YOU HAZARD, FOR IN CHOOSING WRONG I LOSE YOUR COMPANY.

THEREFORE FORBEAR A WHILE — I COULD TEACH YOU HOW TO CHOOSE RIGHT, BUT THEN I AM FORSWORN.

SO WILL YOU MAKE ME WISH A *SIN*.

I SPEAK TOO LONG, BUT 'TIS TO **STAY** YOU FROM ELECTION.

LET ME **CHOOSE**, FOR AS I AM, I LIVE UPON THE RACK.

UPON THE **RACK**, BASSANIO? AY, WHERE MEN ENFORCED DO SPEAK **ANYTHING**.

LET ME TO MY FORTUNE — AND THE CASKETS.

SO MAY THE OUTWARD SHOWS BE LEAST THEMSELVES. THE WORLD IS STILL *DECEIVED* WITH ORNAMENT...

THEREFORE, THOU *GAUDY GOLD*, HARD FOOD FOR MIDAS, I WILL NONE OF THEE.

NOR NONE OF THEE, THOU *PALE* AND COMMON *DRUDGE* 'TWEEN MAN AND MAN.

WHAT FIND I HERE?

FAIR **PORTIA'S** COUNTERFEIT!

THE PAINTER HATH WOVEN A GOLDEN MESH TO **ENTRAP** THE HEARTS OF MEN.

YET LOOK HOW FAR THIS **SHADOW** DOTH LIMP BEHIND THE SUBSTANCE.

FAIR LADY!

GIDDY IN SPIRIT, STAND I DOUBTFUL WHETHER WHAT I SEE BE TRUE, UNTIL *CONFIRMED*, SIGNED, RATIFIED BY YOU.

YOU SEE ME, LORD BASSANIO, SUCH AS I AM. I WOULD NOT WISH MYSELF MUCH BETTER...

YOU SAW THE MISTRESS, I BEHELD THE MAID. YOU LOVED, I LOVED.

I GOT A PROMISE OF THIS FAIR ONE HERE TO HAVE HER LOVE, PROVIDED THAT YOUR FORTUNE ACHIEVED HER MISTRESS.

IS THIS TRUE, NERISSA?

MADAM, IT IS.

OUR FEAST SHALL BE MUCH HONOURED IN YOUR MARRIAGE.

BUT WHO COMES HERE? LORENZO AND HIS INFIDEL! AND MY OLD FRIEND, SOLANIO!

AND I HAVE REASON FOR IT.

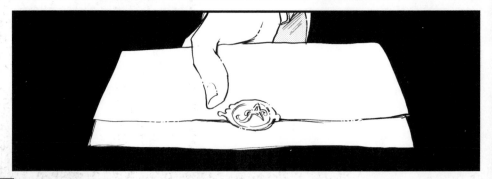

THERE ARE SOME CONTENTS IN YON PAPER THAT STEAL THE COLOUR FROM BASSANIO'S CHEEK.

BASSANIO, I AM HALF YOURSELF, AND I MUST FREELY HAVE THE HALF OF ANYTHING THAT THIS PAPER BRINGS YOU.

O SWEET PORTIA! HERE ARE *UNPLEASANT* WORDS.

BESIDES, IF HE HAD THE MONEY TO DISCHARGE THE JEW, HE WOULD NOT TAKE IT. TWENTY MERCHANTS, THE DUKE HIMSELF, HAVE ALL *PERSUADED* WITH HIM...

BUT *NONE* CAN DRIVE HIM FROM HIS BOND.

I HAVE HEARD HIM SWEAR THAT HE WOULD RATHER HAVE ANTONIO'S *FLESH* THAN *TWENTY TIMES* THE VALUE OF THE SUM THAT HE DID OWE HIM.

WHAT SUM OWES HE THE JEW?

THREE THOUSAND DUCATS.

WHAT! NO MORE?

PAY HIM *DOUBLE* SIX THOUSAND, AND THEN *TREBLE* THAT, BEFORE A FRIEND SHALL LOSE A HAIR THROUGH BASSANIO'S FAULT!

FIRST GO WITH ME TO CHURCH AND CALL ME *WIFE,* THEN AWAY TO VENICE TO YOUR FRIEND!

BUT LET ME HEAR THE LETTER OF YOUR FRIEND.

I PRAY THEE HEAR ME SPEAK.

I'LL NOT BE MADE A *FOOL* AND *YIELD* TO CHRISTIAN INTERCESSORS. I'LL HAVE NO SPEAKING.

I *WILL* HAVE MY BOND.

I'LL FOLLOW HIM NO MORE WITH BOOTLESS PRAYERS. HE SEEKS MY LIFE.

I AM SURE THE DUKE WILL NEVER GRANT THIS FORFEITURE TO HOLD.

THE DUKE CANNOT DENY THE COURSE OF *LAW*.

FOR THE COMMODITY THAT STRANGERS HAVE WITH US IN VENICE, IF IT BE DENIED, WILL MUCH *IMPEACH* THE TRADE AND PROFIT OF THE CITY.

THESE GRIEFS HAVE SO BATED ME THAT I SHALL HARDLY SPARE A POUND OF FLESH TOMORROW TO MY BLOODY CREDITOR.

PRAY GOD BASSANIO COME TO SEE ME PAY HIS DEBT, AND THEN I CARE NOT.

133

I AM SORRY FOR THEE. THOU ART COME TO ANSWER AN **INHUMAN WRETCH** UNCAPABLE OF PITY.

I HAVE HEARD YOUR GRACE HATH TAKEN GREAT PAINS TO QUALIFY HIS RIGOROUS COURSE, BUT HE STANDS OBDURATE.

NO **LAWFUL** MEANS CAN CARRY ME OUT OF HIS **ENVY'S** REACH.

I AM ARMED TO SUFFER WITH **QUIETNESS** OF SPIRIT THE **RAGE** OF HIS.

SHYLOCK,
THE WORLD THINKS,
AND I THINK SO TOO,
THOU'LT SHOW THY
MERCY MORE STRANGE
THAN IS THY STRANGE
APPARENT CRUELTY.

I HAVE SWORN
TO HAVE THE DUE
AND FORFEIT OF
MY BOND.

IF YOU *DENY* IT,
LET THE DANGER LIGHT
UPON YOUR *CHARTER*
AND YOUR CITY'S
FREEDOM.

YOU'LL ASK ME WHY I RATHER CHOOSE TO HAVE A WEIGHT OF CARRION FLESH THAN TO RECEIVE THREE THOUSAND DUCATS.

IT IS MY HUMOUR.

SO CAN I GIVE NO REASON MORE THAN A *LOATHING* I BEAR ANTONIO. ARE YOU *ANSWERED*?

THIS IS NO ANSWER TO *EXCUSE* THY *CRUELTY*.

I AM NOT BOUND TO *PLEASE* THEE WITH MY ANSWER.

WHY DOST THOU **WHET** THY KNIFE SO EARNESTLY?

TO **CUT** THE FORFEITURE FROM THAT **BANKRUPT** THERE.

CAN NO PRAYERS PIERCE THEE?

NO, **NONE** THAT THOU HAST **WIT** ENOUGH TO MAKE.

I STAND HERE FOR **LAW**.

THIS LETTER FROM BELLARIO DOTH COMMEND A *YOUNG* AND *LEARNED* DOCTOR TO OUR COURT. WHERE IS HE?

HE ATTENDETH HERE TO KNOW WHETHER YOU'LL ADMIT HIM.

WITH ALL MY HEART.

THE JUSTICE OF THY PLEA, IF THOU FOLLOW, THIS STRICT COURT OF VENICE MUST NEEDS GIVE SENTENCE AGAINST THE MERCHANT THERE.

I *CRAVE* THE *LAW* — THE PENALTY AND FORFEIT OF MY BOND.

IS HE NOT ABLE TO DISCHARGE THE MONEY?

YES, *TWICE* THE SUM.

ARE THERE BALANCE HERE TO WEIGH THE FLESH?

I HAVE THEM READY.

HAVE BY SOME SURGEON, SHYLOCK, TO STOP HIS WOUNDS, LEST HE DO **BLEED TO DEATH.**

IS IT SO NOMINATED IN THE BOND?

YOUR FRIEND REPENTS NOT THAT HE PAYS YOUR DEBT.

FOR IF THE JEW DO CUT BUT *DEEP* ENOUGH, I'LL PAY IT INSTANTLY WITH ALL MY *HEART*.

ANTONIO — *LIFE* ITSELF, MY *WIFE* AND *ALL* THE WORLD, I WOULD SACRIFICE THEM ALL TO THIS DEVIL, TO DELIVER YOU.

YOUR *WIFE* WOULD GIVE YOU *LITTLE THANKS* FOR THAT IF SHE WERE BY TO HEAR YOU MAKE THE OFFER.

I HAVE A WIFE WHOM I LOVE.

I WOULD SHE WERE IN *HEAVEN*, SO SHE COULD ENTREAT SOME POWER TO CHANGE THIS *CURRISH* JEW.

'TIS WELL YOU OFFER IT BEHIND HER BACK. THE WISH WOULD MAKE ELSE AN *UNQUIET* HOUSE.

THESE BE THE CHRISTIAN HUSBANDS!

I HAVE A DAUGHTER — WOULD ANY OF THE STOCK OF BARABBAS HAD BEEN HER HUSBAND, RATHER THAN A *CHRISTIAN!*

WE TRIFLE TIME. PURSUE *SENTENCE.*

TARRY A LITTLE. THERE IS SOMETHING ELSE.

THIS BOND DOTH GIVE THEE NO JOT OF **BLOOD**. THE WORDS EXPRESSLY ARE "A POUND OF FLESH".

IF THOU SHED **ONE DROP** OF CHRISTIAN BLOOD, THY LANDS AND GOODS ARE, BY THE LAWS OF VENICE, CONFISCATE UNTO THE STATE.

MARK, JEW. O LEARNED JUDGE!

SOFT! NO HASTE!

HE SHALL HAVE NOTHING BUT THE **PENALTY.**

AN **UPRIGHT** JUDGE, A **LEARNED** JUDGE!

THEREFORE, PREPARE TO CUT OFF THE FLESH. SHED **NO BLOOD,** NOR CUT THOU LESS NOR MORE, BUT **JUST** A POUND OF FLESH.

IF THE SCALE DO TURN BUT IN THE ESTIMATION OF A HAIR, THOU **DIEST,** AND ALL THY GOODS ARE **CONFISCATE.**

WHY PAUSE?
TAKE THY
FORFEITURE.

GIVE ME MY
PRINCIPAL AND
LET ME GO.

I HAVE IT
READY FOR
THEE.

HE HATH *REFUSED*
IT. HE SHALL HAVE
MERELY *JUSTICE*
AND HIS BOND.

IF IT BE PROVED AGAINST AN ALIEN THAT BY DIRECT OR INDIRECT ATTEMPTS HE SEEK THE *LIFE* OF ANY CITIZEN,

THE PARTY 'GAINST WHICH HE DOTH CONTRIVE SHALL SEIZE *ONE HALF* HIS GOODS.

THE *OTHER HALF* COMES TO THE PRIVY COFFER OF THE STATE...

AND THE OFFENDER'S *LIFE* LIES IN THE *MERCY* OF THE DUKE ONLY.

NAY, TAKE MY LIFE AND *ALL!*

YOU TAKE MY LIFE WHEN YOU TAKE THE *MEANS* WHEREBY I LIVE.

WHAT *MERCY* CAN YOU RENDER HIM, ANTONIO?

SO PLEASE THE COURT TO QUIT THE FINE FOR ONE HALF OF HIS GOODS, I AM CONTENT.

TWO THINGS PROVIDED MORE. THAT HE PRESENTLY BECOME A *CHRISTIAN*.

THE OTHER THAT HE RECORD A *GIFT* OF ALL HE DIES POSSESSED UNTO HIS SON LORENZO AND HIS DAUGHTER.

HE SHALL DO THIS, OR ELSE I DO RECANT THE PARDON THAT I LATE PRONOUNCED HERE.

ART THOU CONTENTED? WHAT DOST THOU SAY?

I AM CONTENT.

CLERK, DRAW A DEED OF GIFT.

I PRAY YOU, GIVE ME LEAVE TO GO FROM HENCE. I AM **NOT WELL**. SEND THE DEED AFTER ME AND I WILL SIGN IT.

GET THEE GONE, BUT DO IT.

ANTONIO, **GRATIFY** THIS GENTLEMAN, FOR IN MY MIND YOU ARE MUCH BOUND TO HIM.

I AND MY FRIEND HAVE BY YOUR WISDOM BEEN THIS DAY ACQUITTED OF **GRIEVOUS** PENALTIES...

IN LIEU WHEREOF THREE THOUSAND DUCATS, DUE UNTO THE JEW, WE FREELY COPE YOUR COURTEOUS PAINS WITHAL.

AND STAND **INDEBTED** IN LOVE AND SERVICE TO YOU EVERMORE.

AND I, DELIVERING YOU, AM SATISFIED, AND THEREIN DO ACCOUNT MYSELF WELL PAID.

I PRAY YOU, *KNOW* ME WHEN WE MEET AGAIN. AND SO I TAKE MY LEAVE.

TAKE SOME REMEMBRANCE OF US AS A TRIBUTE.

GIVE ME YOUR GLOVES, I'LL WEAR THEM FOR YOUR SAKE.

AND, FOR YOUR LOVE, I'LL TAKE THIS *RING* FROM YOU.

DO NOT DRAW BACK YOUR HAND. YOU IN *LOVE* SHALL NOT *DENY* ME THIS.

THIS RING, GOOD SIR? ALAS, IT IS A *TRIFLE.* I WILL NOT SHAME MYSELF TO GIVE YOU THIS.

I WILL HAVE NOTHING ELSE BUT *ONLY THIS.*

THERE'S MORE DEPENDS ON THIS THAN ON THE VALUE.

MY LORD BASSANIO HATH SENT YOU THIS **RING** AND DOTH ENTREAT YOUR COMPANY AT DINNER.

THAT CANNOT BE.

...

HIS RING I DO ACCEPT MOST THANKFULLY.

FURTHERMORE, I PRAY YOU SHOW MY YOUTH OLD SHYLOCK'S HOUSE.

COME, GOOD SIR, WILL YOU SHOW ME TO THIS HOUSE?

THE MOON SHINES BRIGHT.

IN SUCH A NIGHT AS THIS, WHEN THE SWEET WIND DID GENTLY KISS THE TREES...

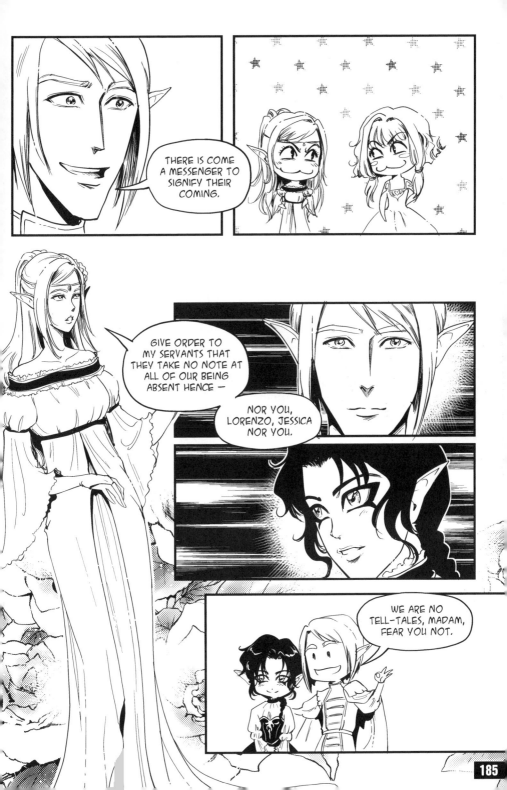

I GAVE MY LOVE A *RING*...

AND MADE HIM *SWEAR* NEVER TO PART WITH IT...

GULP

AND HERE HE STANDS.

I DARE BE SWORN *HE* WOULD NOT PLUCK IT FROM HIS FINGER FOR THE *WEALTH* THAT THE WORLD MASTERS.

GRATIANO, YOU GIVE YOUR WIFE TOO UNKIND A GRIEF.

I WERE BEST TO CUT MY LEFT HAND OFF AND SWEAR I *LOST* THE RING DEFENDING IT.

SWEET PORTIA, IF YOU DID KNOW HOW *UNWILLINGLY* I LEFT THE RING, YOU WOULD ABATE THE STRENGTH OF YOUR *DISPLEASURE*.

NERISSA TEACHES ME WHAT TO BELIEVE — SOME *WOMAN* HAD THE RING!

NO, BY MY HONOUR! NO WOMAN HAD IT, BUT A CIVIL *DOCTOR*, WHICH DID REFUSE THREE THOUSAND DUCATS OF ME.

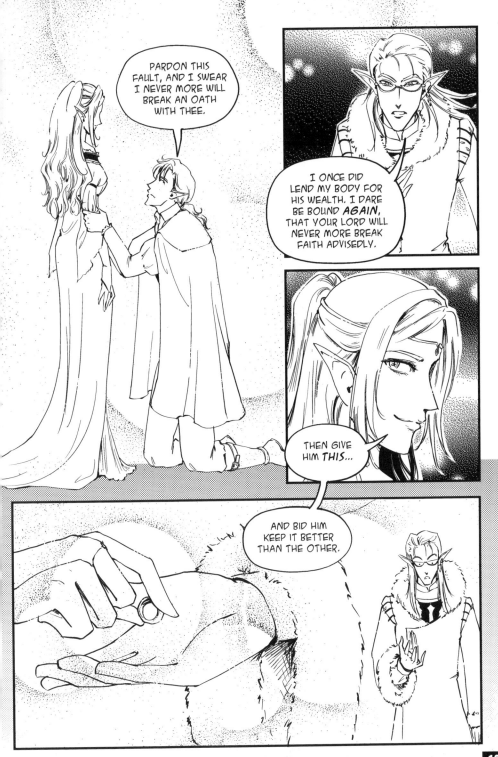

PARDON THIS FAULT, AND I SWEAR I NEVER MORE WILL BREAK AN OATH WITH THEE.

I ONCE DID LEND MY BODY FOR HIS WEALTH. I DARE BE BOUND *AGAIN*, THAT YOUR LORD WILL NEVER MORE BREAK FAITH ADVISEDLY.

THEN GIVE HIM *THIS*...

AND BID HIM KEEP IT BETTER THAN THE OTHER.

ANTONIO, I HAVE BETTER NEWS IN STORE FOR YOU THAN YOU EXPECT.

UNSEAL THIS LETTER. THERE YOU SHALL FIND THREE OF YOUR ARGOSIES ARE RICHLY COME TO HARBOUR SUDDENLY.

I AM DUMB.

WERE YOU THE DOCTOR AND I KNEW YOU NOT?

WERE YOU THE CLERK THAT IS TO MAKE ME CUCKOLD?

LET IT BE SO. MY NERISSA SHALL BE SWORN, WHETHER TILL THE NEXT NIGHT SHE HAD RATHER STAY...

OR GO TO BED NOW, BEING TWO HOURS TO DAY.

BUT WERE THE *DAY* COME...

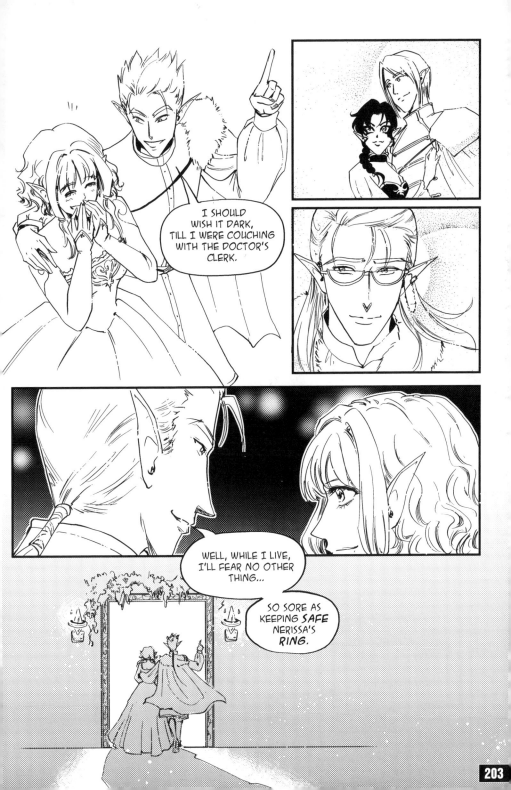

Bassanio, a virtuous but spendthrift gentleman of Venice, seeks to woo and marry Portia, a rich heiress living in nearby Belmont. But he needs money in order to compete with his rival suitors, and approaches his close friend, the merchant Antonio, for a loan. Since all his own wealth is tied up in a large cargo of goods at sea, expected home soon, Antonio agrees to borrow the sum himself from the Jewish moneylender Shylock. Resentful of the prejudice he has previously endured, Shylock nevertheless agrees to lend Antonio the money on the frivolous condition that if Antonio fails to pay it back after three months, he must permit Shylock to cut a pound of flesh from his body. Antonio signs a bond to that effect, and the deal is settled.

The terms of Portia's marriage have been determined by her late father's will: each of her suitors must choose between three symbolic caskets (made of gold, silver, and lead) – on pain of remaining single ever afterwards if they make the wrong choice, and this has deterred a series of worthless chancers, as Portia's maidservant Nerissa reminds her. To their relief, when the Prince of Morocco, and later the Prince of Aragon, take the test, they both fail, each rejecting the leaden casket in favour of, respectively, the showier gold and silver ones.

Meanwhile, Shylock's clownish servant Launcelot Gobbo has deserted his master to work instead for Bassanio; and Shylock's daughter Jessica, assisted by Bassanio and Gratiano before their departure for Belmont, successfully elopes with their friend Lorenzo during the Venice Carnival, along with a stolen casket of her father's gold and jewels. Shylock rails against his misfortune – but then news comes that all Antonio's ships have been lost at sea. Shylock vows to collect his pound of flesh in revenge.

News of Antonio's imprisonment reaches Belmont in the jubilant aftermath of Bassanio's successful choice of the lead casket, much to the relief of Portia (who has fallen in love with him) – and to Nerissa, who has fallen in love with Gratiano. The couples are betrothed, and both men sworn to wear their fiancées' rings forever. Bassanio and Gratiano hurry back to Venice – closely followed by Portia and Nerissa. Entrusting her home to the newly-arrived Lorenzo and Jessica, Portia disguises herself as a male lawyer from Padua (with Nerissa as her clerk), and appears for the defence at Antonio's trial. But what can Portia possibly say against the terms of Shylock's legally binding "pound of flesh"? And what can Bassanio say when the triumphant lawyer asks nothing for payment – except his engagement ring?

A BRIEF LIFE OF WILLIAM SHAKESPEARE

He learned his craft the hard way. He soon won fame as a playwright with often-staged popular hits.

He and his colleagues formed a stage company, the Lord Chamberlain's Men, which built the famous Globe Theatre. It opened in 1599 but was destroyed by fire in 1613 during a performance of *Henry VIII* which used gunpowder special effects. It was rebuilt in brick the following year.

Shakespeare was a financially successful writer who invested his money wisely in property. In 1597, he bought an enormous house in Stratford, and in 1608 became a shareholder in London's Blackfriars Theatre. He also redeemed the family's honour by acquiring a personal coat of arms.

Shakespeare's birthday is traditionally said to be the 23rd of April – St George's Day, patron saint of England. A good start for England's greatest writer. But that date and even his name are uncertain. He signed his own name in different ways. "Shakespeare" is now the accepted one out of dozens of different versions.

He was born at Stratford-upon-Avon in 1564, and baptized on 26th April. His mother, Mary Arden, was the daughter of a prosperous farmer. His father, John Shakespeare, a glove-maker, was a respected civic figure – and probably also a Catholic. In 1570, just as Will began school, his father was accused of illegal dealings. The family fell into debt and disrepute.

Will attended a local school for eight years. He did not go to university. The next ten years are a blank filled by suppositions. Was he briefly a Latin teacher, a soldier, a sea-faring explorer? Was he prosecuted and whipped for poaching deer?

We do know that in 1582 he married Anne Hathaway, eight years his senior, and three months pregnant. Two more children – twins – were born three years later but, by around 1590, Will had left Stratford to pursue a theatre career in London. Shakespeare's apprenticeship began as an actor and "pen for hire".

Shakespeare wrote over 40 works, including poems, "lost" plays and collaborations, in a career spanning nearly 25 years. He retired to Stratford in 1613, where he died on 23rd April 1616, aged 52, apparently of a fever after a "merry meeting" of drinks with friends. Shakespeare did in fact die on St George's Day! He was buried "full 17 foot deep" in Holy Trinity Church, Stratford, and left an epitaph cursing anyone who dared disturb his bones.

There have been preposterous theories disputing Shakespeare's authorship. Some claim that Sir Francis Bacon (1561–1626), philosopher and Lord Chancellor, was the real author of Shakespeare's plays. Others propose Edward de Vere, Earl of Oxford (1550–1604), or, even more weirdly, Queen Elizabeth I. The implication is that the "real" Shakespeare had to be a university graduate or an aristocrat. Nothing less would do for the world's greatest writer.

Shakespeare is mysteriously hidden behind his work. His life will not tell us what inspired his genius.

MANGA SHAKESPEARE®

EDITORIAL

Richard Appignanesi: Text Adaptor

Richard Appignanesi was a founder and co-director of the Writers & Readers Publishing Cooperative and Icon Books where he originated the internationally acclaimed *Introducing* series. His own best-selling titles in the series include *Freud*, *Postmodernism* and *Existentialism*. He is also the author of the fiction trilogy *Italia Perversa* and the novel *Yukio Mishima's Report to the Emperor*. Currently associate editor of the journal *Third Text* and reviews editor of the journal *Futures*, his latest book *What do Existentialists Believe?* was released in 2006.

Nick de Somogyi: Textual Consultant

Nick de Somogyi works as a freelance writer and researcher, as a genealogist at the College of Arms, and as a contributing editor to *New Theatre Quarterly*. He is the founding editor of the *Globe Quartos* series, and was the visiting curator at Shakespeare's Globe, 2003–6. His publications include *Shakespeare's Theatre of War* (1998), *Jokermen and Thieves: Bob Dylan and the Ballad Tradition* (1986), and (from 2001) the *Shakespeare Folios* series for Nick Hern Books. He has also contributed to the Open University (1995), Carlton Television (2000), and BBC Radio 3 and Radio 4.

ARTIST

Faye Yong

A former pianist, Faye left Malaysia to pursue an Illustration degree in the UK. She graduated with First Class Honours in Visual Communication (Illustration) from Birmingham City University in 2008. She is now a professional illustrator and comic artist specializing in digital art. Her main influences and inspirations are from digital painting, concept art, fantasy, fashion as well as manga. Her first graphic novel *Murphy's Law* was published in 2008 by Sweatdrop Studios. Faye came third in the hotly contested Rising Stars of Manga UK & Ireland 3 in 2008 and won the People's Choice Award in the same year. *Merchant of Venice* is Faye's second full length graphic novel.

PUBLISHER

SelfMadeHero is a UK-based manga and graphic novel imprint, reinventing some of the most important works of European and world literature. In 2008 SelfMadeHero was named **UK Young Publisher of the Year** at the prestigious British Book Industry Awards.

OTHER SELFMADEHERO TITLES:

EYE CLASSICS: *Nevermore, The Picture of Dorian Gray, The Trial, The Master and Margarita, Crime and Punishment, Dr. Jekyll and Mr. Hyde.*

SELF MADE HERO

www.selfmadehero.com